CONTENTS

ANNELI THE
ART HATER

Also by Anne Fine

How to Write Really Badly
The Country Pancake
The Angel of Nitshill Road
Bill's New Frock
Press Play
Scaredy Cat
Countdown
Design-a-Pram
A Sudden Puff of Glittering Smoke
A Sudden Swirl of Icy Wind
A Sudden Glow of Gold

Telling Tales – An Interview with Anne Fine

For older readers
The Summer House Loon
The Other Darker Ned
The Granny Project
The Stone Menagerie
Very Different

Anne Fine
Children's Laureate

ANNELI THE ART HATER

EGMONT

First published in Great Britain 1986
by Methuen Children's Books Ltd
Reissued 2002
by Egmont Books Limited
239 Kensington High Street, London W8 6SA

Text copyright © Anne Fine 1986
Illustrations copyright © Vanessa Julian-Ottie 1986
Cover illustration copyright © Lee Gibbons 2002

ISBN 1 4052 0186 X

10 9 8 7 6 5 4 3 2

A CIP catalogue record for this title
is available from the British Library

Printed and bound by
Cox & Wyman, Reading, Berkshire

CHAPTER ONE

'More pink, dear, don't you think?'

Anneli didn't, but was too polite to say so.

Miss Pears dabbed once or twice at Anneli's painting.

'There! Much, much better. But you'll need more.'

Anneli scowled as Miss Pears turned her back and started mixing more pink. She hated painting. She hated anything to do with art. She loathed messing with clay and smudging with pastels. She disliked greasy crayons and despised collages. She hated all non-toxic glues and tatty little scraps of coloured material and dried pasta shells and leftover Christmas wrapping paper. She was bored stiff by all those interminable discussions about what everyone was going to do.

'What a good idea, Henry! Who else has an idea? Anyone? No one?'

She hated the chaotic sharing out of all

the horrid stuff that they were going to do it with.

'Bags the red!'

'I asked *first*!'

'No, you did *not*!'

'Swap the green lace for half those beads? Please? Pretty, pretty *please*?'

'He asked *first*!'

'No, he didn't!'

She hated all discussion of themes.

'Winter? We had that last week. Sunshine? Not enough yellow and orange scraps left, I'm afraid. Any more bright ideas? Henry? Aliens from Outer Space? *Good*, Henry. That should get rid of some of this tin foil.'

And whatever the theme chosen in the end, Anneli hated doing it. She'd toil away, getting it finished as soon as possible, but she resented all Miss Pears' encouraging remarks as she made her way round the room, rescuing a warped drawing of a cat for one person, mixing an awkward red-brown colour for another, breaking up fights. She hated having

to show the finished product to her friends afterwards, especially to Henry. She hated carrying it home, whatever it was. She hated having to stand there while her mother praised it, however awful it was, and stuck it on the fridge door for the whole world to see. She hated having to look at it every morning over her crunchy cereal while it got grubbier and grubbier, until the sellotape at last dried up and mercifully it fell off and slid out of sight under the fridge, the final resting place for all Anneli Kuukka's artistic endeavours.

To be fair, she hated other people's art more. She walked down school corridors with her eyes averted from all the bright splashes of colour pinned up on the walls. When they did children's art on the television she clutched her belly, pretended to vomit and switched straight off. Class trips to the local art gallery made her squirm.

'Look at that! Isn't that *breath-taking*? Have a good peep at the brush work. Don't we all wish that we could paint like *that*?'

'No.'

'Yuk.'

'Well, he got *paid*.'

Yes, Anneli Kuukka was a real art hater. Miss Pears turned back with the freshly mixed pink and Anneli wiped the scowl from her face, but still it sat in her heart as she dabbed and poked and scraped about with the bald old paintbrush, trying to use up a bit of the extra pink anywhere there was room so as not to seem rude, longing for the bell to ring and release her.

Brrrrrrr!

'Heavens! The bell! We haven't even begun putting away. Oh, dear me!'

Anneli sighed. It happened every week. Everyone knew the bell was going to ring, and nobody warned her. They all preferred ten minutes of clearing up the art materials to ten extra minutes of whatever might come after. It was a gamble. By afternoon, Miss Pears only sporadically fell in with the time-table. You might be lucky and miss maths. But, then again, you might miss wonderful, peaceful, almost-as-good-as-being-back-home silent reading. It all depended on how much strength Miss Pears had left.

And she was pretty old. Towards the end of the afternoon it started showing more. Wisps of grey hair escaped from her bun and straggled down the back of her neck. Her woollies sagged on her like bean sacks. Her stockings wrinkled round her legs. She always seemed to shrink an inch or two between morning register and afternoon bell.

Today she looked completely worn out. It came as no surprise to Anneli to see her sink on to her chair well before the clearing up was completed. A stream of commands came from behind her desk, laced with advice and praise for the co-operative, scoldings and threats for all the rest. She kept her feet up all the same.

'And now I want to talk to you about the new Art Room Appeal.'

Groans. Mutters. The surreptitious sliding out of desks and on to laps of books and comics. What did she want to go on about that again for? Hadn't they given enough of their pocket money, and wheedled enough out of their parents to build a new Art Room out of ivory bricks and equip it with diamond-studded easels and ermine paint-rags? Perhaps there were plans to fill the paint pots with molten silver and gold? They'd been collecting long enough . . .

'Even more money . . .'

Anneli the Art Hater

Oh, not again! The giant jam jar on Miss Pears' desk had been filled up and emptied four times. Art Room Appeal receipts curled over one another on the notice board. They'd reached the class target three times already, but Miss Pears was mad on painting, and wouldn't stop.

'. . . not to go running to your parents, who have more than enough strains on their purses, but think of things to do yourselves. Can anyone think of any ways of making a little money? No one? Henry?'

Anneli slumped down on her folded arms and shut her eyes. She heard good old Henry droning on about baking cakes to sell in break-time, and sweeping up dead leaves (not that it was the time of year for that, but Miss Pears didn't seem to notice), and looking for precious old forgotten things in attics. Then Henry's drone turned into the sound of waves lapping a sunlit shore, and she was miles away, knee-deep in salty water, her arms speckled with gritty golden sand, her eyelids spangled with glistening water drops.

Surina brought her back by passing a tattered *Beano* across her to Owen, and asking:

'What are you going to do, then?'

'What?'

'To make money. What are you going to do?'

'Nothing.'

'Nothing?'

'Oh, I don't know. I'll think of something.'

And think she did, all the way home. It wasn't so easy. She almost began wishing she'd listened to Henry. After all, if money were so very easy to come by, someone smart would already have scooped it up. All very well to talk of baking cakes to sell at break-time. Anneli's mother came home worn out. Teaching stiff, shy beginners to dance is no joke. Anneli could imagine only too easily the look of pain her mother would turn to the ceiling if Anneli fixed stern eyes on her and told her it was baking time.

What about Jodie? Jodie and Josh lived in the top half of the house, and just as Anneli's mother looked after little Josh whenever Jodie had to go back and work in the evenings, so Jodie was supposed to be in charge of Anneli when her mother taught her dance classes at the Leisure Centre. Would Jodie help her bake the cakes? No doubt she would; but she'd be bound to let Josh help – she was his mother, after all – and Josh was only two and a half. He was a messer. He'd drop bits of egg shell in the cake mixture, and fiddle with the oven temperature dial while they were cooking, and spoon the runny icing over the tops while the cakes were still too hot to take it. He'd put the cherry halves on upside down. He'd ruin the whole batch. Anneli knew it.

She reached the corner. The towering wrought-iron gates guarding the driveway that led up to Carrington Lodge were padlocked shut, as usual. As usual, Anneli stopped, dropped her school bag and clutched the bars, peering inside. The Lodge was now a children's home, and sometimes, in fine weather, the children could be seen in the gardens, some lying on waterproof rugs on the lawns, some scuttling around in their wheelchairs, some being carried to and fro by paid helpers like Jodie. Anneli liked to wave, if they were there. They always waved back, if they could. They all knew Anneli because Jodie sometimes had to take her and Josh along in order to get to work at all.

But today there was no one in sight. Only the drive and what little could be seen of the long sloping lawns, and the six great holly trees shading the high stone wall behind. No point in hanging about. Anneli picked up her bag and strolled on, into her own street, her thoughts turning back to Henry and his ideas for making money.

Cake baking might be out, but what about the other two ideas? What were they, now? Oh, yes. Sweeping up leaves. Ridiculous! Anneli hadn't seen a dead leaf in months. And looking for precious things in attics.

Anneli sighed, raising her eyes to heaven. Sometimes she really wondered where Henry's

reputation came from. In looking up, she caught sight of Old Mrs Pears' pale face behind the glass of an upstairs window. Mrs Pears waved. As she came up the shared garden path, Anneli waved back, politely feigning a happy smile. When your own teacher's mother lives next door, you don't take chances. Safe in the porch, the smile dropped away like a discarded Hallowe'en mask, and moodily kicking the door open, Anneli walked in.

CHAPTER TWO

Behind the door, Josh was standing on one leg, waiting for her, his thumb in his mouth and the purple velvet cloth to which he'd been attached for as long as Anneli could remember clutched tightly in his fist as usual.

'Hello, Josh.'

''Lo.'

He followed Anneli along the hall and into the kitchen. Here, Anneli put her arms round him and hauled him up until he was high enough to wriggle his bottom on to the table top. He liked to sit there watching her make the afternoon snack for them both. It was her job, and Josh liked watching other people work.

Anneli rooted through the forest of jars in the cupboard.

'Fish-paste or peanut butter?' she asked him.

'Fish-paste. Not beef fish-paste.'

'Beef aren't fish.'

'Are.'

Anne Fine

Anneli couldn't be bothered to argue. The little jars all looked the same. For someone as small as Josh, who couldn't read, there probably wasn't any real difference. It didn't take Anneli long to make the sandwiches. She'd had enough practice. She handed one to Josh and started on the other herself.

'What did you do today at playgroup?'

Josh made a face.

'Had to sing songs.'

'You're lucky,' Anneli told him with feeling. 'I had to paint.'

In a sudden surge of sympathy, Josh held the purple velvet cloth, all spattered with bread crumbs, out towards her. 'It's all right,' Anneli told him. 'It's all over now.'

Josh finished up what was left of his sandwich, then started picking up the bits he'd dropped on the table and eating those.

'Where's Jodie?' Anneli asked him.

He pointed through the kitchen window to where, down at the bottom of the garden, his mother was standing with her finger over the end of the hose pipe, spraying the insides of the dustbins with a forceful jet.

'Go and help Mummy?' Anneli suggested hopefully.

'Help you,' Josh said firmly.

'Go on, then,' Anneli said. 'Help me. Which do you want to do first? Sweep up dead leaves, bake cakes to sell, or find an attic full of precious things?'

Josh looked embarrassed.

'Not got no leaves,' he said. 'Can't cook.'

'Not got no attic, either,' Anneli said bitterly.

Henry's trio of bright ideas had all turned out to be right duds.

'Got an attic,' said Josh.

'Don't be silly. We haven't got an attic.'

'Got an attic.'

'You don't know what an attic is.'

'Do.'

'Don't.'

He stuck his tongue out at her.

'Do.'

Anneli was irritated.

'All right,' she challenged him. 'Show!'

Josh held his arms out. Anneli lifted him down. Pausing only to pick up from the floor a bit of crust he'd dropped, and pop it neatly in his mouth, he made for the door. Anneli followed. It never for one moment occurred to her that Josh had anything at all to show her worth seeing, let alone an attic; but while Jodie stayed out of sight and hearing, cleaning dustbins, she was in charge of Josh, and so she went with him.

He clambered laboriously up the stairs, one by one, gripping the banisters, until he reached the door that separated the top half of the house from the bottom. Anneli pushed it open for him. He walked straight past his own tiny little bedroom, barely larger than a cupboard, and through the room in which Jodie kept her books, her sewing machine, the television and the stereo. He threaded his way between the giant overstuffed armchairs, and grasped the handle on the door to his mother's bedroom.

Anneli the Art Hater

'You'll catch it,' Anneli warned. 'You're not allowed to play in there.'

'Not playing,' Josh insisted. 'Showing.'

He opened the door.

Going into Jodie's room was, Anneli always thought, like stepping in a magical cavern, or going under water suddenly. The glorious silk shawls draped across the window to hide the dark stone wall outside made it glow soft and greeny-blue, like living at the bottom of a goldfish bowl. The room smelt of herbs and flowers and joss sticks. Plants trailed and climbed all over, even inside the grate of the old-fashioned fireplace with blue patterned tiles. Little bells hanging by embroidery silks from the curtain rail were jingling softly in the draught from the window. The floor was bright with rugs, the bedspread a riot of patchwork. And scattered all over, everywhere, on everything, were pretty things: rings that dazzled, bangles that caught the light, earrings that sparkled; small painted jewel boxes, tiny enamelled beads, gleaming glass pots, brass

dishes overflowing with strange foreign coins. The walls were bespattered with vivid postcards, and a huge wide floppy straw hat with trailing scarlet satin ribbons hung from the bed post. Everywhere you looked was something you longed to try on or touch or stroke, or take the lid off and peep inside.

Small wonder that Josh was forbidden to play here.

'Go on, then,' Anneli prompted nastily. 'Show.'

To her astonishment, Josh gathered himself up and dived under the bed. He disappeared beneath the hanging folds of patchwork counterpane.

She heard his muffled voice.

'Come *on*.'

Catching her breath, she knelt and followed him.

Under the bed, it was quite dark and very dusty. Anneli sneezed several times. When she recovered, it was to find that Josh had stuck his purple cloth in her face.

'There,' he said. 'Bless you.'

Anneli pushed the cloth away.

'Where's this great attic, then?' she asked unpleasantly. She was exceedingly uncomfortable. Her hair was catching in the metal bedsprings overhead, and pulling. She was bent double. It was too dark to see a thing, and Josh's feet were digging firmly in her stomach.

'There,' Josh proclaimed.

'Where? I can't see a thing!'

'There!'

Josh patted her all over till he found one of her hands. He took it in his, and pulled it across until it touched the wall behind the bed. Anneli spread her fingers wide, and felt. Strange. Very strange. It didn't feel like wall. It felt like wood. It felt like painted wooden panelling.

Anneli put out her other hand. Using her fingertips, she traced on the wall the outline of a tiny wooden door, no more than two feet high, complete with tiny rounded knob and a little metal catch.

Anneli the Art Hater

'What's behind there, then?'

'Attic.'

'It's just the water tank, silly.'

'Attic.'

'It *can't* be.'

Maybe it could, though. Anneli wasn't certain. It was a door. Surely no one would go to all the trouble of putting it there unless there were something behind. It might be just a water tank. But, then again, it might be attics.

Only one way of finding out. Anneli made her mind up fast. There was no point in putting if off. All that would happen was that her imagination would have time to run riot about the dark or the cobwebs or all the awful things the door might hide. If she was ever going to open it and look, it must be now.

She scrambled out from under the bed. Seizing Josh by a leg, she pulled. He came out sliding on a rug.

'You go on down. I'll follow you.'

'Tea time? asked Josh, ever hungry, ever hopeful.

'Maybe,' said Anneli vaguely. 'Tell Jodie you've seen me and I'll be along in a minute.'

Josh stayed cross-legged on the rug for a few moments, practising the message.

'Seen Anneli. 'Long in a minute.'

Then he got to his feet and pottered off towards the door.

Before his back had even disappeared from sight, Anneli had dived beneath the bed again. This time she found the little door without any trouble. Her fingers tightened round the knob. She took the deepest breath.

'Here goes,' she told herself. 'Here goes.'

CHAPTER THREE

The knob turned easily. Anneli heard the tiny catch click as it slid back. She gave the door a tentative pull but nothing happened. She pulled again, harder. Stubbornly the door refused to budge an inch. Anneli tried pushing. The little door swung open so easily it gave her a fright.

A curious musty smell swept out. It was a strange odour of ancient dust and shy spiders and the driest of haybarns. There was nothing slimy about it at all. Nothing dank and disgusting. And that, at least, was a relief. Not daring to delay any longer, Anneli poked her head through the door. Nothing with creepy long legs fell in her hair. Nothing furry and fast scuttled across in front of her.

So far, so good.

She peered into the darkness. Only the slimmest needles of light fell from above her head through the cracks in two or three slates.

In them, dust motes were spinning. It was a moment or two before she could make out that the floor was rough boards, and above was the sharply sloping underside of a roof.

Anneli peered to the side. On her left, huge and squat like a vast sleeping monster, lay the water tank. A pipe led in at one end, another led out at the other. The lid was crooked. Anneli shuddered, dreading to think what might have crept along the edge, slipped in and drowned, and still be lying at the very bottom. She'd never drink from the bath taps again.

She looked the other way. Darkness. It was impossible to see how far, if any distance at all, it would be possible to crawl. For all that she could tell, the little passage under the roof might come to a dead end only a few feet away, or might go on forever. It was too dark to see.

And there was not enough time right now to find out. At any moment Jodie might rush up the stairs and burst in in search of a clean blouse or a pair of tights without holes. She wasn't likely to spend the whole evening wearing exactly what she wore to clean dustbins. Anneli had better make herself scarce.

She backed out hastily and shut the little door with care. Poking her head out from under folds of patchwork, Anneli listened anxiously for sounds of footsteps on the stairs. Nothing. Well, good. She scrambled over the rugs to the door. Here she stood up and brushed the dust marks from her clothing before going down. By the time Anneli strolled in the kitchen again, a couple of moments later, she looked for all the world as if she had just spent a calm and profitable twenty minutes alone in her bedroom, doing her homework.

Jodie was the vilest of moods, banging the pans down on the oven, and rattling drawers ferociously in search of the elusive chopping knife. Josh stood in the doorway, holding his purple cloth to his cheek, watching.

Anneli sidled past him and took a chair at the table.

'Don't sit there,' Jodie snapped. 'You're in my way. Sit on the other side.'

Anne Fine

Anneli moved round. An acrid smell rose from the pan. Cursing, Jodie turned her back and stirred furiously.

Anneli walked her fingers surreptitiously over the table to the small heap of chopped celery, and stole a sliver.

'Put back that celery,' warned Jodie in her dangerous voice.

'You're only guessing.'

'Guessing or not, you put it back.'

'What's eating you?'

Jodie looked round.

'Nothing,' she said. 'Nothing at all. Oh, I just had the very finest day. First, I'm dead broke and the cheque doesn't come from his father.' She pointed her thumb at Josh, who sucked his own even harder. 'And then some expensive bit of the car packs in on my way back from Sainsbury's. Then I drop half the shopping and most of what I drop rolls down the street. Then I'm locked out. Then, while I'm climbing in our upstairs window, Miss Pears' old mother is looking out of hers next

door and telling me our dustbins are smelly. Then I clean dustbins and break two nails.'

'Bad day.'

'Bad day.'

'Was Old Mrs Pears all horrid?'

'No,' Jodie said, regretfully. 'If she'd been horrid, I could have left the dustbins for another day. She was most polite. She was so polite that I was hanging half in and half out of the window for ten minutes while she tried to get round to saying it.'

'And *did* they smell bad?'

'Smell bad? Honey, they *stank*. I don't know how the poor old lady stood it so long. They were sitting right under her window, stinking so bad you'd think they might have got up and walked away and cleaned themselves. It took forever to rinse them out. And now I'm behind with supper, and it's poor Helen's Bellyful Tuesday.'

Anneli grinned. On Tuesdays her mother came home so frayed and exhausted from teaching three belly dancing classes in a row –

Anneli the Art Hater

Beginners, Intermediate and Advanced – that she called it Bellyful Tuesday and it was a toss-up whether she fell asleep before or during supper.

'And you? Will you be staying in tonight?'

'Not me, honey.' Suddenly Jodie looked grave. 'I have a most important meeting from seven till nine.'

'More bad day?'

'I hope not,' Jodie said with real feeling. 'Oh, do I hope not!'

Seeing the look on her face, Anneli hoped not, too. But seven till nine? Perfect!

Everything worked out as Anneli hoped. By seven her mother was fast asleep in an armchair, not having even made it through her own imitation of Mrs Hyams' first attempt at belly dancing. Jodie had put Josh to bed, and gone off to her meeting. Anneli had found her torch – and several other long-lost articles – under her bed, and borrowed two batteries from Jodie's radio. She'd changed into a dirty shirt and jeans she'd dug in the laundry basket to find. She was quite ready. All she needed now was a little more courage.

For this time the hole under the roof looked even more spooky. Great shuddering yellow rings of torchlight illuminated odd cracks and crannies, but gave no more sense than darkness had of the exact shape of the space behind the little wooden door. Anneli crept in. As the torch trembled in her hand, the rafters seemed to swoop down on her, and away again, as though the creepy hole itself were breathing, as though she were inside the belly of some huge living animal with rafter ribs. If she'd not spent so much time keying herself up, she would have turned and fled. As it was, she kept on, shuffling forward on her knees towards that lump of shadow at the end that might be a corner she could crawl round and keep on going.

She inched her way forward. Just as her nervousness was lessening, behind her there came a noise, a huge and echoing clang that startled her so much the torch slipped from her sweating fingers. It rolled away across the boards, the eerie circles of light it threw ahead billowing and rolling. Down from the rafters came fearsome echoes of the appalling clang. Anneli felt sick with terror. She shut her eyes, too panic-stricken even to move.

Then, suddenly, another noise took over. The sound of rushing, filling water.

Of course! The water tank in action!

Anneli kept her eyes shut till she was absolutely sure. In this enclosed space, the sound seemed so enormous that it was hard to be convinced that this was just another household noise. To ring round the rafters like that, it surely must at least mean a fractured water pipe, flooding, some awful kitchen or bathroom disaster to startle her mother out of sleep.

But no. Already the hissing rush was slowing to a trickle, then tiny spurts, then droplets running after one another fast, and then, at last, just the occasional drip that sounded roundly and wetly and hollowly, as if in some ancient cavern underground. Anneli pulled herself together. The crisis was over. She reached out for her torch, and, grasping it tightly, she carried on.

The perplexing lump of darkness turned out to be, not a corner leading to further passages, but a kind of alcove, set back like those narrow brick bays inside a railway tunnel into which workmen flatten themselves as a train rattles past. Anneli flashed her torch. In its pulsing yellow cone of light, the bricks and plasterboard in front of her looked perfectly solid. Anneli was relieved that there were no fresh terrors tucked away to be faced. But so much for all her planning and bravery. So much for Henry's brilliant idea. Something precious to sell in an attic! How stupid!

Bitterly disappointed, Anneli sat down and leaned back against the alcove.

There was the loudest of clicks, and then a hideous grating noise. Whatever Anneli was leaning against was giving way. She struggled to regain her balance. A little door, no larger than the one she'd crawled through earlier, was swinging open. After the dim glow from her torch, the bright light on the other side temporarily blinded her, and she was quite unable to save herself. She tumbled backwards, head over heels, catching her elbows on the frame of the doorway and landing on theadbare carpet that scraped her knees. Tears pricked behind her eyes. She blinked them shut. But when she opened them again, what was there right in front of her, not more than two or three inches away, but the most hideous face that Anneli had ever seen, glaring at her with fierce hatred.

CHAPTER FOUR

Anneli shut her eyes tightly again, out of sheer terror, and waited for whoever it was to pounce and savage her.

But nothing happened. The moments passed. She could not even hear the sort of heavy, aggressive breathing that she associated with a look of such awful fierceness. Nothing. Just silence, absolute silence. No sound of breathing at all, in fact, unless she were to count her own fast nervous panting. Had she imagined it all in the great shock of tumbling sideways through the hole? Had she seen what she thought she saw?

She flickered her eyelids open the tiniest fraction. Not enough for anyone watching to think she was looking at them. Just enough to let the smallest crack of light seep in between her eyelashes and let her peep a second time.

That face! Still there! But something so odd about it . . .

Anneli the Art Hater

Anneli's eyes widened. Without being able to prevent herself, she cried out loud:

'What a great cheat!'

It was a painting.

Life-size, and stuck right in her face, it had fooled her in the jitteriness of the moment into thinking it real. But it was just a painting, propped up and facing where she fell.

'What a great fizzing *cheat*!'

And then from the other side of the room:

'What's a great fizzing cheat?'

The unexpected voice alarmed Anneli even more than first sight of the painting. The blood ran cold in her veins. She couldn't answer.

She heard it again.

'*What's* a great fizzing cheat? Who *are* you? Come on out from behind there, so I can see you. What's going on?'

Anneli Kuukka was no chicken. She'd never found that trying to avoid trouble got her out of it, or made it any easier when it came. She'd never believed in ghosts, and she was

pretty philosophical about tangling with human beings, even exasperated ones into whose rooms she fell, uninvited and filthy dusty. So gathering herself together, she scrambled to her feet, and peered with burgeoning curiosity over the large gold frame of the painting.

There, standing in the middle of the room and staring back with equal curiosity, was Old Mrs Pears.

'Anneli!' said Mrs Pears. 'How very neighbourly of you to drop in.'

Anneli grinned, a little sheepishly.

'Are you hurt? Are you horribly bruised? That was a thump and a half.'

Anneli prodded experimentally at the worst bits.

'Not too bad,' she admitted. 'I'll be all right.'

'Did you bring Josh along with you? Or is he mislaid somewhere in the roofing system?'

'No,' Anneli said. 'Josh is in bed. It's only me. And I was hoping to find something precious.'

Mrs Pears looked about the room, and made

a vague but gracious gesture of invitation.

'Oh, no!' said Anneli hastily. 'I didn't mean from you!'

'One has to bear in mind,' said Mrs Pears, speaking softly, as though to herself and not to Anneli, 'there's precious and precious. Precious to sell and precious to keep.' She turned back. 'In this room, I'm afraid, there's mostly the latter.'

Anneli didn't know how to begin to answer. Confused, she looked about her. The room itself was, she saw at once, the mirror image of the room she'd crawled from, Jodie's bedroom. There was the same bow window, the same two matching cupboard doors, even the same old-fashioned fireplace with blue patterned tiles.

But in every other respect, the room could not have looked more different. Where Jodie's room was filled with cosy chairs and the brass bed and the pine dressers on which she kept all her pretty things, this room was far more sparsely furnished. A narrow bed, no wider than Anneli's, lay against one wall. A desk and chair stood under the window. A high-backed armchair sat by the fireplace, facing a large brass coal scuttle. Where Jodie's floor was covered brightly with rugs, here was spread only a drab grey thin carpet.

And the rest was paintings. Nothing but paintings. Paintings hanging on every spare inch of wall, and propped above the mantelpiece, and leaning in stacks against the cupboard doors, and laid flat on the desk. Dozens of paintings in dozens of frames. Discreet slim frames and florid golden ones, serious black frames and heavy ugly ones, even delicate carved frames. Everywhere you looked in the room were drawings and paintings – snarling wild animals, blossoming trees, fast flowing rivers, beautiful women in long white dresses lifting their parasols against the harsh sunlight, men fighting battles, women weeping, a little girl sitting on a bench nursing a black and white rabbit.

Art. Everywhere you looked. Nothing but art.

'Did you *buy* all of them?' demanded Anneli, far too aghast at the thought of such a massive waste of money to remember her manners.

'Lord, no,' said Mrs Pears. 'My brother painted them.'

'*All* of them?'

'Every last one.'

'What *for*?'

Mrs Pears stared at Anneli, and then asked civilly:

'Anneli, do you know very much about art?'

'Nothing,' said Anneli.

'You don't draw, or paint, or go regularly to galleries, or look at books of prints?'

'We slosh about a bit on Tuesday afternoons,' Anneli offered helpfully. 'But that's about it.'

'And do you enjoy it?'

'Not much,' said Anneli, then added with a flash of truthfulness: 'Actually, I hate it.'

Mrs Pears waved her hands around in the air, as though seeking delicately for the right words.

Anneli the Art Hater

'So, when you say: "What for?", what you mean is: "Why did your brother waste his time painting when he could have been doing something else entirely?"'

Anneli blushed.

'I suppose so.'

'And not what many others ask, which is: "Why, when he clearly had talent, did your brother spend so much time copying other artists' paintings?"'

'Is that what he was doing?'

Mrs Pears sighed.

'It was.'

Anneli looked around her, and breathed out slowly.

'He certainly copied an awful lot of paintings.'

'He certainly did.' Mrs Pears let herself down into the chair by the fireplace. 'And he certainly copied a lot of awful paintings, too.' She shut her eyes, as if to blot out the memory of some of the worst. She looked exhausted suddenly, and for the first time Anneli noticed the strong resemblance between Old Mrs

41

Pears and her daughter, when a hard morning's teaching had sent Miss Pears' stockings wrinkling round her knees, and her woollies sagging. It was a bit embarrassing, so Anneli turned her attention back to the paintings.

'But why?'

'He wanted money.' Mrs Pears sighed. 'My brother wanted as much money as he could lay his hands on.'

'What for?'

'For his Running-Away Box.'

Anneli was momentarily shocked. A Running-Away Box? It sounded little sort of desperate.

'Was your brother very unhappy?'

There was a silence. Mrs Pears sat with her head tilted against the chair back, her eyes still closed, her hands neatly folded in her lap. Finally she said:

'Be a dear, Anneli. Run away home. Come back tomorrow and I'll find you something precious to sell.'

Anneli the Art Hater

Anneli thought to protest. She hadn't meant to fall in like this on Mrs Pears, and beg for something to sell. It was the rudest thing to do. Her mother would be furious if she found out. But just as she opened her mouth to start explaining all this, she caught sight of the tear that had squeezed out between Mrs Pears' closed eyelids, and was tracking unchecked down her cheek.

Without a word, Anneli bent to pick up her torch from where it had rolled to a halt against a painting of a petunia in a pot. She clambered back through the little door, pulling it shut behind her. The torch, thank heaven, still worked, though the batteries were fading. But somehow the short crawled journey through the dark roof space did not seem frightening any longer. Perhaps because Anneli now knew the tunnel both started and ended somewhere quite safe, even the shadows beyond the glimmering rings of torchlight were now more curious than threatening.

As Anneli emerged from under the bed, the

tiny brass bells that hung from Jodie's curtain rail were swaying and tinkling fiercely. Outside, dark clouds scudded across a deepening inky sky. The wind was getting up. The silk shawls billowed like galleon's sails. Anneli stepped across and pulled down the window. Just as she did so, her mother appeared in the doorway.

'You beat me to it,' Helen said. 'I heard it rattling from downstairs.'

'I thought it might wake Josh.'

Anneli followed her mother back down the stairs. Soon her apple and cocoa were waiting, her hot water bottle filled, her duvet plumped up on her bed. Anneli climbed in. Her library book was satisfactory: not too chewed up on the outside or too disappointing on the inside. But still she couldn't read. She couldn't concentrate. Her eyes skimmed over the words, but inside her head all manner of things were scrambling for her attention, distracting her from the story. Mrs Pears, all those paintings, the brother with his Running-

Anneli the Art Hater

Away Box, that quiet little tear. It was a mystery, and once there was any sort of puzzle in her life, Anneli could never rest until she had solved it.

When Helen came in to switch off the light, Anneli laid down the book without regret.

'Good day, sweet?'

'It was Tuesday,' Anneli reminded her mother, scowling.

'So?'

'So we had art.'

'And what did you paint?'

Anneli thought back. She could still see perfectly clearly in her mind's eye any number of Mrs Pears' brother's paintings – the one that scared her out of her wits, the lovely lady with the frills and the lap dog, the terrified horse – but the large sheet of paper that she herself had worked on for most of the afternoon was no more than a misty blank.

'Something stupid. I can't remember.'

'You never can. You're a real art hater, Anneli. I don't know why I keep bothering to ask you!'

Anne Fine

Her mother left the room, yawning. Anneli lay back. She listened to the evening's clatter through the half-open doorway. She could identify each sound, however odd or rare. She knew if her mother was filling the teapot or drinking whisky and soda. She was familiar with the sound of rubbish being put out, or the cat being let in. She could distinguish the rustle her mother made turning over the pages of the newspaper from the sound the cat made when it nested inside it. And if anyone phoned, she could tell from the tone of her mother's voice who it was.

She'd listened to these sounds as long as she could remember. Usually they lulled her to sleep, but tonight was different. Though she was tired, her mind was racing, and she was still awake when Jodie let herself in.

'Well?' she heard Helen asking. 'How did your meeting go?'

Anneli heard Jodie sigh. Then:

'Terrible. Terrible. They're going to close the pool.'

Anneli the Art Hater

Anneli jack-knifed upright in bed. She couldn't believe it! Close the swimming pool at Carrington Lodge? Why, swimming was the only real pleasure some of those children had! They did lots of it, too. It was good for their bodies. On the days Jodie had taken Anneli and Josh along with her, Anneli had seen children who could barely walk straight or manage their wheelchairs moving around in the water as though there were almost nothing whatever the matter with their spines or their muscles or their disobedient legs.

Helen was equally shocked.

'Close the pool? What? For ever?'

'No, not for ever. Just for a year or so.'

'A year or so! That might as well be for ever for some of those children!' Helen said bitterly.

'I told you it was a terrible meeting.'

Anneli heard the sofa springs sagging as Jodie settled.

'It seems that pool's quite ancient. The bottom's giving way, the heating unit is too old for safety, the changing rooms are going mouldy, and the lights need rewiring. They've decided to repair the whole lot all in one go; but none the less it will take months and months.'

'But, Jodie, what about the children? Why can't they use the pool in town?'

'They can. And they will. But only at certain times of day. And since the minibus can only hold four wheelchairs at one time, there won't be much swimming for anyone this year.'

'Unless they get another minibus.'

'On top of all the repairs to the pool?'

'Have a collection!'

'We only just finished the *last* collection. People round here aren't *made* of money.'

The two of them relapsed into what Anneli guessed to be gloomy silence. More than a little despondent herself, she rolled over and bunched the duvet up over her head. Cracked pools and mouldy changing rooms. Only one minibus. Art rooms. Everyone needed money for something. She simply didn't want to hear another word. She'd think about it tomorrow . . . tomorrow . . .

CHAPTER FIVE

Tomorrow turned out to be the oddest day, and not one on which Anneli found time to think much at all. When she reached school in the morning, she found Henry doubled over the gates, waiting for her, shrieking the news.

'Miss Pears is off.'

'Off?'

'Not coming to school.'

'That's never happened before. Perhaps she's feeling sick.'

'Perhaps she's ill.'

'Perhaps she's *very* ill.'

'Perhaps she's dying.'

'Perhaps she's dead.'

'Perhaps she's buried.'

'Don't be so silly. Who are we getting instead?'

'No one. There isn't anyone, so they're splitting us up. Everyone else is having five of us. We're to be helpers.'

'Teaching babies the ABC?'

'You won't be any use, then. You don't know yours yet.'

The insults kept up through the ringing of the bell, and standing in line. Anneli was smart. Grabbing Henry tightly, she fought her way right to the very front with him, reckoning that the deputy head would come down to split them into fives. If Mrs Fleming had any sense at all, she'd pick all the quiet goody-goodies queuing at the front, dying to get into school, to join her in the infant class. And since Anneli liked Mrs Fleming and didn't mind infants, she was determined that she and Henry would get into Mrs Fleming's pack of five.

The strategy paid off. Soon she and Henry were being swept away in a tide of little people.

'I feel like Gulliver among the Lilliputians,' Henry remarked.

Mrs Fleming, it was clear, had no idea what to do with the five she had picked. She certainly didn't want helpers. When Henry asked wistfully, 'Can't we go round the class and tutor your reluctant readers?' Mrs Fleming shuddered.

'Certainly not,' she said, 'I've only just got some of them going. I can't have you lot putting them off with all your bad habits.'

'What *can* we do, then?'

'I'm already bored.'

'So am I.'

'I've been bored ever since we got in here.'

'So have I.'

'Are there no real books in here at all?'

Mrs Fleming looked around the room desperately, searching for an idea. Anneli watched with sheer horror as her eyes settled on the six easels in the painting corner, the aprons, the jam jars filled with bright poster paints.

'Art,' she said firmly. 'That'll be nice.'

'No, it won't,' Henry said loyally. 'Anneli hates art.'

'*Painting*! Not painting *again*!'

'We had art yesterday.'

Anneli the Art Hater

'Painting? All *day*?'

'On those silly easels?'

'I'm certainly not wearing one of those bibs!'

Mrs Fleming lifted her hand for silence.

'You five can stay in that corner together and paint quietly,' – she paused – 'or I can send up for a set of long division cards.'

The complaining quietened to a sullen muttering. As Henry took it upon himself to distribute the brushes, even the muttering died away. Contained fits of whispered squabbling broke out instead.

'I can't paint with this. This brush is *bald*. I might as well paint with my *fingers*.'

'I've seen your work. I thought you did.'

'This brush has exactly seven bristles left in it.'

'Let *me* count.'

'Careful!'

'Whoops. Sorry.'

'Now there's only six!'

Anneli dragged her easel backwards until it stood right behind Henry's, and she could see exactly what he was doing. She waited while he stared at his large blank sheet of paper, deciding what to paint. Henry never drew anything in pencil first. He said that the lines always spoiled it after. He simply thought for a long while instead.

As she stood watching, Anneli found herself

filling with curiosity. What was he going to paint? Which colour would he begin with? Would his brush strokes be bold and slashing, or dotty and delicate? She waited, burning with impatience, for him to start.

Then, at last, Henry dipped his brush into a jar of light blue. Anneli did the same, moving as far as possible like an action replay on the television. Henry drew his brush firmly across the sheet of paper. With a growing feeling of interest, Anneli followed suit.

She'd never taken to art, but Anneli was nothing if not resourceful. It was going to be a very long morning. Remembering Mrs Pears' brother, she'd give copying other artists' work a good try.

At break time, everyone crowded round the two finished paintings.

'Which one is Henry's?'

'This one. It's got his name on it.'

'But that one has, too.'

Anneli grinned. She had enjoyed herself

enormously. She'd found it fascinating, and for the first time in her life she'd had a paintbrush in her hand without feeling irritable. From time to time during the morning, Henry had stepped back to admire her work, and now it was finished he did so again.

'That's very good.'

'You did it.'

'But you painted it.'

'But it's your painting.'

Henry screwed up his face.

'Funny, that. Whose is it, then?'

'Yours.'

'Hers.'

'Mine.'

'His.'

'Both of ours.'

Everyone had an opinion on the matter, and voiced it often, at length and loudly, until Mrs Fleming ordered them out into the playground.

Henry asked Anneli:

'Was it difficult to do?'

Anneli the Art Hater

'Not really,' Anneli said, 'once I got into the swing of painting like you do. I found it was easier when I didn't try to keep up. When you were stabbing away at those tree tops I couldn't stab as hard and as fast as you did in case you weren't making them the shape I thought. So I stopped till you'd finished, and then did them all in a rush, like you, after.'

'They came out just the same,' Henry admitted admiringly.

'Almost,' said Anneli, ruthlessly self-critical. 'Not quite.'

Henry leaned over and pointed to her version of the painting.

'See that red there. It's wrong.'

'Your red had white in it. It wasn't like mine. I kept trying to add just the right amount to get it exact.' Anneli ran her finger over the red of her barn roof. 'But it didn't come quite right until I got here.' She pointed again. 'I tried going back and painting over, but that made it look too thick, so I had to stop.'

'You can see where you've gone over it twice.'

Anne Fine

'Only because you've been told.'

'Maybe.'

'The worst,' said Anneli, 'was the geese.'

'Yes, geese *are* difficult to paint,' said Henry complacently.

'It wasn't that,' Anneli assured him. 'It's just that I could hardly bring myself to do them. It was such a *mistake*, don't you think, sticking them all over the grass and sky like that, flapping their wings.'

For a moment, Henry just stared. But by the time he'd leaped to his feet and started after her, she was already half way towards the sanctuary of the girls' lavatories, and both the paintings had been whipped away by the wind.

By afternoon, Miss Pears was back in school, looking quite well if a little tired. The rest of the day passed quickly enough, what with all the morning's work to be done as well as a bit more. The final bell took Anneli by surprise.

She couldn't wait to get home, feed Josh,

and get away next door to hear more about Mrs Pears' brother. Her respect for him had increased considerably over the morning. Reeling off Henry's geese was one thing. Copying real artists was quite another.

Josh, of course, had to be in his slow-coach mood.

'What do you want in your sandwich?'

'Salad cream.'

'Salad cream and what?'

He took forever to answer. She tapped her foot impatiently.

At last:

'More salad cream.'

'You can't have that.'

There were strict rules about the sandwich combinations. Jodie and Helen made them up. They were occasionally relaxed a little, or tightened up a lot; but even at their most lax they'd never included salad cream sandwiches with extra salad cream.

To try and speed him up a little, Anneli did her imitation of Miss Pears getting snappy:

'I'm waiting, Josh.'

Josh stared interminably at the light-fitting on the ceiling. Finally he said:

'Just salad cream.'

'That's not allowed.'

'Salad cream, fish-paste and honey.'

Jodie or Helen would have said: 'Are you quite *sure*?' to Josh; but Anneli never bothered. So far as she was concerned, if the sandwich he wanted wasn't explicitly against the rules, then he could have it and good luck to him. However digusting they were, he ate them. But though he glared at her balefully, she still spread the fish-paste more thickly than either the salad cream or the honey. That was in the rules. She stuck the second slice of bread on top and handed the sandwich to him. He took only one bite before carefully peeling the two halves apart and peering inside. The fish-paste and salad cream and honey had mushed together. It looked revolting, Anneli thought – all messy splodges running into one another like that painting above the door to

Anneli the Art Hater

the Ladies in the local art gallery, or the infant's picture that won the poster competition for the Art Room Appeal Fund.

The Art Room Appeal Fund . . . At this reminder of the need to raise money, Anneli was even more impatient to get away next door and see what Mrs Pears had found that was precious-to-sell but not so precious-to-keep that it couldn't be parted with.

Barely able to contain herself until Josh had finished his last churning mouthful – he wasn't yet allowed to eat anywhere else but the kitchen – she steered him as fast as he would let her towards the stairs and Jodie, and then she slipped off next door.

Anneli rang the doorbell and stamped with impatience, waiting for Mrs Pears to let her inside. Through the lozenge-shaped pane of red glass in the door she could see the old lady descending. She seemed to take as long to get down stairs as Josh sometimes took to get up them.

Mrs Pears seemed astonished that Anneli

had thought to use the front door.

'Sorry to take such an age,' she said. 'I admit to waiting for you upstairs, by the hole.'

Anneli went scarlet.

'I couldn't have come that way in any case,' she mumbled. 'It's right behind Jodie's bed.'

Mrs Pears' face filled with concern.

'Jodie's not poorly, I hope? She's not caught something nasty out of those dustbins? Oh, I should never forgive myself!'

'No,' Anneli said. 'She's pretty miserable about things, but she's not sick.'

'Come in,' Mrs Pears said hastily. 'Come in. Not at all the place to discuss things, a doorstep.'

Anneli followed her in. Mrs Pears led the way into the sitting room, and sat on the sofa. She patted the space at her side, and Anneli sat down. A tray of tea things lay in front of them on a low table, and there were chocolate biscuits.

'Sugar in your tea?'

'I'm not allowed,' Anneli said bitterly. 'I'm

not allowed tea very often, either.'

If she was expecting shock and sympathy, she was quite out of luck. Mrs Pears nodded her head with approval.

'Quite right,' she said. 'Quite right. I do so admire this tough new breed of young mothers.'

(She didn't seem to notice how many chocolate biscuits were vanishing, though.)

Anneli told her everything. She told how she lay in bed the night before, unable to sleep, and heard Jodie coming home from her meeting at Carrington Lodge. She told about the cracks in the bottom of the pool and the failing heating unit, the unsafe wiring and the mouldy changing room. She told Mrs Pears how the children so enjoyed their time in the water, and how the pool was going to be closed for a whole year.

'A whole year . . .' The old lady's face softened with memory. 'Why, it took half that to build in the first place!'

Anneli was astonished.

'How do you know?'

'Because I remember very well. I remember quite as clearly as if it were yesterday.'

'Were you there?'

'There? I watched every day, from dawn till dusk. Behind my back, the workmen called me The Shadow.'

'They let you in the garden?'

'It was my garden.'

'*Your* garden?'

'My garden and my pool. The pool was built for me. It even has my initials built in it. When you were visiting, didn't you ever notice the fancy initials on the side of the pool, down at the deep end?'

'Those tiny blue and green tiles?' Anneli recalled treading water and tracing them with her fingertips, wondering about them. Each letter was the size of her hand, so curvy and elegant and old-fashioned, it was hard to be sure which letter it was. 'There was an A, I remember. I loved the curly legs on the A.'

'C. A. M. C-S. That's what the letters are. My name – or, rather, my old name before my marriage: Clarissa Amelia Mary Carrington-Storrs.'

Anneli stared.

'I thought Anneli Sarah Kuukka was a mouthful.'

'Anneli Sarah Kuukka is positively streamline,' the old lady said, 'compared with Clarissa Amelia Mary Carrington-Storrs.'

'And now you're Mrs Pears.'

'And the house in which I grew up is a home for children.'

'But it's a *lovely* house!' Anneli burst out. She remembered so clearly and with such pleasure her few afternoons in its large wild gardens. 'Why did you ever, *ever* leave?'

Mrs Pears sighed and smiled and inspected her fingernails closely.

'Ah,' she said. 'And so we come back once again to the tale of my brother.'

'Tell,' Anneli said. '*Please* tell.'

So Mrs Pears told.

CHAPTER SIX

'When I was young,' Mrs Pears told Anneli, 'we lived at Carrington Lodge. My father built it. He'd made one fortune of his own, and married another, so he was very rich indeed. He ordered that lovely house to be built, and my mother designed the garden. Gardeners did the work, but my mother gave the orders: a summer-house here, a rose-trellis there, an orchard, low privet hedges round the flower beds, tall holly trees to hide the stable wall.' She sighed.

'It's changed a lot. They've taken up the crazy paving and laid down concrete paths for the wheelchairs, and any one of our old gardeners would have a fit if he saw the lawns. But the house is still standing, and you can still almost get lost in the grounds.'

'Oh, yes,' Anneli said. 'I almost have.'

'We were four: my mother, my father, my brother and myself. My brother was called

Tom, and he was older than I. He was away at school most of the time.'

'Who did you play with?'

'No one. There was no one to play with. I wasn't permitted to play with village children. They weren't sufficiently "respectable". I played alone. I wasn't lonely, though. I made up friends, imaginary friends, and played with them.'

'Were you happy?' asked Anneli, remembering Tom's Running-Away Box.

'Oh, I was happy; but my parents were horrified. I can't think why, even now, but they were. They'd watch me sitting on the white benches beside the lawns, offering to share my toys with empty air, or they'd overhear me answering unasked questions, or catch me laughing at nothing with no one, and they became so anxious, so anxious . . .'

'They built the swimming pool, to distract you.'

'How clever you are!'

'Just a guess,' Anneli said modestly.

Anneli the Art Hater

Mrs Pears said: 'Have another biscuit,' before she noticed they'd all gone.

'I sat and watched from the day the first men came to measure and stake out the huge rectangular shape, to the day the last coat of glaze was painted over the tiny little blue and green tiles that spelled my initials. I sat on a bench. I was never allowed to sit on grass in case it was damp and I took a chill. Colds could be dangerous in those days. We sat on the bench – all my imaginary friends and myself – and watched our pool take shape in front of us.'

'Didn't Tom ever watch with you?'

'Oh, no. Even on holidays, Tom was always busy. He'd taken a passion for painting, and whenever he was home he spent all day and evening in the conservatory, painting and painting. He'd leap off the school train acting like someone starved for the smell of oil paint and turpentine.'

'Didn't he paint at school?'

Mrs Pears laughed.

'They hadn't much time for art in Tom's sort of school!'

Privately, Anneli thought this no very bad thing. But she said nothing.

'He snatched up his brushes the moment he came home, and barely laid them down till he left. He painted anything and everything. He even painted me. Do you remember the painting of a girl in frilly skirts sitting on a bench nursing a black and white rabbit?'

'Yes. I saw that one.'

'Well, that was me. I sat still for hours. The rabbit became quite testy, and nibbled me badly.'

'Did you make Tom pay you?'

'*Pay* me?' Mrs Pears raised an eyebrow. 'Heavens! It would never even have occurred to me to hint at the notion.'

'Unless they were paid, no one in my class would sit still to be painted.'

'Even by their own brother?'

'Especially by their own brother.'

Mrs Pears said:

Anneli the Art Hater

'How times do change.' She stared down at the plate of biscuit crumbs, remembering. 'I think that I was very proud to be asked. Usually he painted other sorts of pictures entirely.'

'Sunsets and rivers and battles and petunias and tigers,' said Anneli, recalling some of the paintings upstairs.

'Rivers were fine,' said Mrs Pears. 'There are three rivers within easy cycling distance of the Lodge.'

'No tigers, though.'

'No battles, either. But there were sunsets and petunias. And that's really how the trouble began. Because Father was a little uneasy about Tom's passion for painting. He was a plain man, you understand. He'd mixed with plain men all his life, for all he'd made and married money. And in those days, you know, a plain man didn't think it quite right for his one and only son and heir to spend his days painting pink sunsets and petunias. It made Father most uncomfortable. He thought it girlish.'

'Like thinking it's unladylike for girls to be explorers.'

'Exactly. Though Mother, of course, wasn't anxious about that. She was too busy fretting because her daughter sat on a bench the live-long day watching a hole dug deeper and deeper, and whispering to invisible people.'

'You sat and sat?'

'I sat and sat. And in the end Tom said: "If Clarrie's just sitting on a bench all day anyhow, she can make herself useful and sit for me. I'll paint her." So he carried his easel out to the garden and ordered the maid to look out my frilliest dress. He fetched the most biddable rabbit from the hutch, and began to paint. And since I was determined not to stop watching the workmen, he had to set his easel up beside the hole.'

'Wasn't that in the way?'

'Indeed it was.'

'Didn't the workmen mind?'

'Oh, they minded. But then, as now, a workman would put up with being inconvenienced if he was glad as the day to have work at all, and earn the wage. There's no getting round the fact that both of us were in the way. Tom was nuisance enough with his easel and clutter and fussing about shadows in his way. But I was worse.'

'How? You were only sitting there, after all.'

'But if any one of those poor men stopped and leaned on his spade for a moment, I'd be calling: "Why have you stopped? What's the matter?" It wasn't that I resented their taking a break. It was simply that I feared they'd suddenly come across some snag — impenetrable bedrock, quicksand, a swamp — anything that might prevent my pool being finished. I didn't mean to be forever urging them on. Lord, no. But I suppose I had the same effect on them as if I did. And gradually they became less friendly. Then almost sullen. And towards the end, though they were never actually *rude*, they took to relieving their resentment in quiet little ways.'

'What ways?'

'They'd pretend not to hear when I called out to them. And if they noticed me chattering to my secret friends, they'd mutter: "Soft in the head," and grin and shake their heads, and screw their fingers to their temples. And whenever Tom came over to shake out the frills in my dress they'd smirk a little behind his back, and flex their huge bronzed muscles, and nudge one another knowingly.'

'Making out Tom was a bit of a pansy.'

Mrs Pears stared down at Anneli.

'Well, yes,' she said after a moment's pause. 'I suppose what I'm describing could be phrased that way.'

'That's certainly the way they'd phrase it at our school.'

'Is it, indeed?'

Blushing, Anneli prompted a quick return to the story.

'So the workmen were teasing you both.'

'Just a little. But enough to cause mighty trouble once Father noticed. He stepped out from the yew tree walk one morning without warning. He must have been standing in the shadows for quite some time, watching quietly, as the workmen surreptitiously sniggered and mocked at Tom and myself. But suddenly he strode out into the sunlight, startling everyone, and bellowing with rage.'

'What did he bellow?'

'I've no idea to this day. I was so terrified that not a word went in. All I know is, the workmen crept off with all their tools, scowling horribly. And on the next day there were four different men, and Tom never painted in the garden again.'

'Never?'

'He was forbidden.'

'Forbidden?'

'Forbidden entirely. Father threatened to break his head if ever he caught Tom painting in front of other people again. He meant it, too. Oh, it was quite unreasonable, everyone agreed, even my mother, though she only dared hint as much in a whisper. But it was final. My father was so angered and humiliated by the

Anne Fine

incident that, weeks after, if he so much as came across one of Tom's brushes lying about, he'd snap it in two directly.'

'Did Tom stop painting?'

'Stop painting? Tom? As soon tell wind to stop blowing. He simply set up his easel in his bedroom and started to copy a painting on the wall.'

'Ah,' Anneli said. 'Started to copy.'

This was the bit she wanted to hear.

'That's right. Lots of artists do it. It's most instructive. A way of improving one's own work.'

'I know,' said Anneli. 'I've done it. Mine improved a lot.'

'Yesterday you told me you didn't take very much interest in art.'

'I take a bit more now. Starting this morning.'

Mrs Pears took a deep breath, and continued:

'The house had quite a collection of paintings and drawings. Father bought huge ugly paintings cheap at auctions and hung the horrors all over, and Mother bought lovely delicate drawings from Paris to try to distract attention from Father's worst choices. So there was plenty to choose from when Tom wanted something to copy.'

'And he was good at it.'

'Oh, he was very good indeed. He had a gift. He soon became so deft, so skilled, so *good* at copying, that apart from the fact the originals were framed, it was difficult to tell which of two drawings or paintings was which.'

'How *do* you tell?'

After her experience of the morning, the question interested Anneli.

'Tom said: "The longer you look at the real thing, the better and richer and finer it seems and the more life you see inside it. The longer you stare at my copies, the more they seem to shrivel inside".'

'But if they're both the same . . .'

'But they're not. The artist is painting in his own way, just what he wants, from his own soul. He can let go.'

'And the copier can't.'

'Exactly.'

'That was the trouble with my tree tops, then,' muttered Anneli.

Mrs Pears stared.

'I beg your pardon. Did you mention tree tops?'

'Yes,' Anneli said. 'No. Carry on, please. Didn't Tom paint any more for himself?'

'That painting of me on the bench with the rabbit was one of the last two real paintings that Tom ever did.'

'Can I go up and look at it again?'

'By all means,' Mrs Pears said. 'I'll come too. Take my arm.'

It took forever to get up the stairs. Like Josh, Mrs Pears had to take steps one at a time, and clutch the banisters to keep her balance. Anneli burned with impatience. She'd never thought she'd be longing to get a second look at a painting. But she could hardly wait to get up in the room and sort through the canvasses till she found it again.

It was in the corner, behind one just the same size of a middle-aged man with a

cavalier hat and merry eyes. Compared with that one, it seemed a dreamy sort of painting. Gently, Anneli slid it out of the stack and leaned it against the leg of the desk, in the light from the window.

The little girl seated on the bench in the sunlight looked anxious and forlorn. Her face was pale under her bonnet, and slim white fingers dug in the fat rabbit's fur in a rather desperate way, as if she feared that he, like everybody else, might hop away from her at the first opportunity. A slight flush on her cheeks hinted to Anneli that the dress must have been a horror to wear – stuffy and cumbersome. And there was something else. A little ring of rash circled Clarissa Amelia Mary Carrington-Storrs' narrow neck.

Anneli said:

'The lace round the neck of that dress was all prickly!'

'So it was! How I remember! However did you know?'

Anneli leaned forward and pointed to the

tiny rash ring.

'My heavens!' said Mrs Pears. 'You're sharp enough to be an art historian!'

'Is that a job?'

'It certainly is.'

'That might be fun,' said Anneli. 'See what people had for supper four hundred years ago.'

'And if they had rats running round the kitchen.'

'And if they wore any clothes in bed.'

'And what they kept for pets. The Spanish princesses had real live dwarves for pets. They're in the portraits.'

'That's *terrible*.'

'*They* didn't think so. You can work out what people thought from a painting. Once, women's bodices were worn very low, and people painted them that way. Then people who lived later were so shocked by the very same paintings that they went to all the trouble to pay artists to paint extra ringlets of hair falling over the bare skin, to cover it up.'

'You wouldn't have needed any extra

ringlets,' said Anneli. 'Your dress was almost up to your ears. Why do the trees behind look funny like that?'

'Tom never managed to finish the painting.'

'What a waste. Was he angry with your father?'

'Angry? He was so angry he started the Running-Away Box. He said he wouldn't stay in the house a week longer than he had to. He was so desperate to make a start saving, he even bullied me into giving him my two gold sovereigns in return for his cricket bat and his stamp collection.'

'But you didn't play cricket!'

'I didn't collect stamps, either. But he was desperate. And he was my brother.'

Anneli wiped the look of utter disbelief and contempt off her face. If being brought up rich enough to have a private swimming pool built for you meant you were also brought up to wear heavy prickly dresses in a heatwave and knuckle under a selfish bossy brother without even thinking to grumble, she'd give up the pool and take T-shirts and Josh.

'How much were two gold sovereigns worth?'

'They were valuable even then. Nowadays, they're precious.'

'Precious,' repeated Anneli. 'That's what I'm after, something precious.' Her face fell. This need to spend her time thinking of ways to raise money kept nibbling at her general good spirits. 'It's a real pity your brother spent it all, running away.'

'Ah, that's just the mystery,' said Mrs Pears. 'It seems he didn't.'

'He didn't?'

'As far as we know, Tom never took any of the money with him when he disappeared.'

Anneli could bear it no longer. She reached out and took Mrs Pears' hand in her own. Tugging gently, she steered the old lady towards the armchair.

'Sit down,' she begged. 'Oh, please sit down. Sit down and tell me how Tom ran away.'

CHAPTER SEVEN

It was the swimming pool again, you know. Without that, things might have settled down. But, no. Instead they got worse. And, once again, it was all on account of that pool.

By midsummer, the work was finished. It was decided that there should be a party, a sunny daytime picnic party around the newly completed pool. In those days it wasn't all closed in with walls and a roof, as it is now. It was open to the air, and fringed with bushes and climbing plants that the gardeners hastily transplanted from other parts of the grounds to disguise the trampled mud the workmen's boots had stirred up. An awning was slung up over part of the lawn. Trestle tables were laden with wonderful dishes. The champagne flowed. And everybody we knew from miles around was there to celebrate with us, and admire.

Father strode round the gardens, his bushy red beard and whiskers waggling, hearty and welcoming to his guests. Mother stood, pink with pleasure, greeting her friends and relations. The gardens were at their most colourful and flourishing, and everyone was complimenting her on how fine they looked. Ladies strolled about under their sunshades, quarrelling discreetly about the suffragettes in London, who were smashing windows and scuffling with policemen, and chaining themselves to railings, and generally behaving in a most startling fashion in their astonishing fight for the vote. The men stood in groups, discussing the assassination of some Austrian Archduke no one had ever heard of, somewhere in Europe. Small children raced and weaved round shrubbery bushes, hissed at by nannies. And Tom stood at his window upstairs, in shadow, watching. He was in no mood to come down and join the celebration.

'Clarissa,' Mother whispered. 'Run up and tell Tom to join us in the garden at once. These are our guests, and he must take his part in welcoming them!'

Anne Fine

But someone else had spotted Tom standing by the window. She was a tall and elegant young woman, a French cousin of Mother's on a rare visit, wearing a hat drooping feathers as wide as fans. She lifted her long skirts a little at the front, and stepped through the french windows into the house. She made her way through the cool hall and up the staircase, tapping on several doors before she found the room where Tom was standing in front of his easel, gazing thoughtfully out at the gardens, all bright with midsummer blooms and milling finery.

'Tom! 'Ow tall you 'ave grown! You're taller than I!'

Tom was so startled he swung round clumsily, upsetting the little table beside him. On it, a small ink drawing was lying drying, Tom's copy of Mother's most recent purchase.

As the table tipped, the drawing slid off. It floated slowly through the air, and Madame Germaine reached out and caught it in flight.

She turned it the right way up, and looked

at it. Then she inspected it with more care. Then she looked up.

'Why, Tom! This is a Larrien, *n'est-ce-pas*?'

Tom grinned with pride.

'It's mine.'

'Yours, Tom? You mean you *own* it? It's not your father's?'

Tom laughed.

'It certainly isn't my father's. It's mine.'

'*Ma foi*!' she said, staring. 'A Larrien all of your own!'

Tom said: 'How do you know that it's a Larrien?' He meant: 'How can you be so sure it's not just a copy of a Larrien?'; but Madame Germaine would have none of that.

''Ow do I *know*? I know something about Joseph Larrien, I can tell you. I've visited 'is studio in Paris. I've seen all 'is exhibitions in London. I know enough to know it's definitely by Larrien and it's quite exquisite. I love it. I want it. Indeed, I *must* 'ave it, and I'll give you this much for it right 'ere and now, Tom!'

And she emptied her little bead purse upside down on the table.

'Can it be worth more than all that?' she demanded.

Tom stared.

'No,' he said, very slowly. 'It's not worth more than all that. That's for sure.'

'Then it is *mine*.'

Tom tried. He did try. His voice was dry and choked, and the money lying on the table amounted to twenty times what was in his Running-Away Box after weeks of hard saving. But still he managed to say:

'It's not a Larrien. It's just a copy.'

Madame Germaine swept the pile of money closer towards Tom with the flat of her hand, and snatched up the drawing.

'Nonsense!' she cried. 'It's quite as good a Larrien as ever I've seen. You're only trying to back out of a deal. But it's mine now, and thank you, my darling!'

And, kissing him warmly on both cheeks, she swept out.

Anne Fine

'By the way,' she called back. 'Little sister Clarrie is lurking behind this door. She daren't come in and tell you what she's been sent all the way up 'ere to say – that your mother wants you out in the garden, all party manners, *tout de suite.*'

And she was gone.

Tom spread out his hands. They were dead white, and trembling. He stared at them. Then he lifted his head, and he whispered in horror:

'Clarrie, I think I've just become an art forger.'

'A life of crime,' breathed Anneli. 'Started by accident!'

Mrs Pears said:

'It was quite terrible. It went from bad to worse. I was sworn to absolute secrecy, but I suffered terribly from the guilt. Things were so different then, you know. Now, getting away with something like that is seen as rather clever, and anyone who spends a fortune on a painting and doesn't even know exactly who painted it is not so much sympathised with as laughed at. But it was different in those days. All cheating was seen as terrible. Dishonourable. A total disgrace. And he was my brother. I lay awake at nights and sobbed and sobbed.'

'Did no one notice?'

'Notice? My dear, war had begun. The murder of that little Archduke we'd never heard of tipped all of Europe into war. The men joined regiments, the women set to work. The suffragettes took up nursing. The Great War had begun, and everything changed overnight, or so it seems to me, looking back. No one had time to notice a little girl sobbing herself to sleep at nights, or a young lad drawing and painting as if there were no tomorrow.'

'You couldn't make him stop?'

'It was as if the devil had got into him. You've no idea. He worked night and day, copying drawings and paintings. He practically went into business, persuading an uncle on leave from his regiment to pick up a block of very old French paper. He told him French paper was better, and old paper had dried out better; and Uncle had far too much on his mind, fighting a war, to guess Tom wanted it because it was the sort of paper Larrien would have used. He never forgave himself, after, for being so gullible. And while the war dragged on and on, Tom sat in the old schoolroom churning out Larriens as if they were . . .'

'Lavatory paper?'

'Well, not quite that, perhaps. But he produced them one after another. He forged a letter from Father to his school, announcing his late arrival one term, and slid away to London. Nobody noticed. Everyone was far too preoccupied with all the bad news from the war front to pay attention. There, Tom found someone who swallowed, or pretended to swallow, his fanciful story about family debts and the forced sale of paintings and drawings. And from then on, Tom sent a steady stream of forgeries to London.'

'And all the money went into his Running-Away Box.'

'All of it.'

'Must have been a huge box.'

'Not so big. Gold sovereigns are surprisingly small, you know. Not much larger than shillings.' She noticed Anneli's blank face and tried again, moving a decade or so nearer the present: 'More like a ten pence.'

'You could get plenty of those in a box.'

'The box was made of rosewood, and lined inside with purple velvet. It had a silver clasp and a silver lining on all the corners, and set in the lid was a little silver shield, engraved with T. W. H. C-S.'

Anneli looked blank.

'Thomas William Hubert Carrington-Storrs.'

'*Hubert?*'

'Yes, Hubert. Why?'

'No reason.' Anneli straightened her face. 'Go on.'

Anne Fine

'So the months passed. News of the war got worse and worse. As more and more men were killed, more were needed. Even my father and all my uncles joined up. My mother's sister came to live with us, and a strange life we had then, all women and children and very old men. And then . . . and then . . .'

'And then . . .'

Mrs Pears picked at the folds of her skirt.

'And then Madame Germaine came down to stay with us.'

'Trouble?'

'Trouble indeed. It wasn't *all* her fault, mind you. For Tom was getting a little bit cocky. Everyone said so. They'd no idea why, but they could see it. I knew why. It was the secret life, swelling his head. He found the risk exhilarating. It was a glamorous thing to do, you see, to produce work that was the equal of a grown man's, or seemed to be. He'd even seen one of his own forgeries hanging in an art gallery, for all to see! Imagine! He told me, in the strictest confidence, he felt quite shocked! And Father was no longer around to keep him firmly in place. So when Madame Germaine arrived – '

'And kissed him on both cheeks!'

'Yes, quite. He thought himself a fellow indeed. And when she fluttered her eyelashes and talked about those brave, *brave* men at war – '

'Oh, no!'

'Oh, yes. My brother, who was tall for his age, took it into his head to go for a soldier.'

'But he was *far* too young! Surely they wouldn't let him join up!'

'Boys as young as twelve sneaked into that war. The need for soldiers was desperate. Nobody looked too closely or asked too many questions.'

'Madame Germaine must have felt terrible!'

'Perhaps she did. Perhaps she didn't. I've no idea. Neither of my parents ever spoke a word to her again.'

The meaning of this took a moment or two to sink in. Mrs Pears sat quietly, picking at folds in her dress with her fingers. At last, Anneli broke the silence.

'How long?'

'Eight months,' said Mrs Pears. 'We waited eight grey, endless, anxious months before the news came of his death in battle. Father was grieved, but proud. Mother was bereft. She wrote to Father that she couldn't bear to pace the same rooms, weep in the same garden where she'd watched her dear Tom growing and playing. As soon as the war ended and Father came home, we sold up everything.'

'They kept the paintings, though. They never guessed.'

'That Tom had become a forger? No, they never guessed. The paintings were locked up, out of sight, never looked at, and I never said a single word. He meant so much to them I couldn't bear to mar his memory.'

'And then . . . ?'

'And then, one day, months after, when the worst of the tears had dried and we could sometimes smile again, the last painting arrived.'

'Tom's last real painting?'

'Tom's last real painting. Entrusted to a fellow soldier who had been wounded so badly it took him that many months to recover enough to seek us out, and give it to me.'

'To you?'

'It was for me. The note with it said so. It said: "*For Clarrie. All I own. Best Love, Tom*".'

'What was it like?'

'See for yourself.'

Mrs Pears pointed up above the fireplace.

CHAPTER EIGHT

From the moment she first saw the painting, Anneli knew that there was something mysterious about it.

But what on earth could be peculiar about a boring old painting of the view of Carrington Lodge from the gates, the same view Anneli saw every single school day when she dropped her bag and poked her head between the bars in order to wave at the children, if they were there: the view of the top of the long sloping lawn and the seven great holly trees shading the high stone wall behind.

What could be mysterious about that? Nothing.

Anneli tried to keep the disappointment out of her voice.

'It's very pretty,' she said. 'It looks almost exactly the same as it did. He painted it well.'

But Mrs Pears didn't seem to be listening. Perhaps she was tired after all the remembering.

Anneli looked at her watch.

'I should go home now. Thank you for tea. Can I help you down the stairs again?'

Mrs Pears shook her head.

'You've quite forgotten,' she said, 'the "something precious" I was going to find you. I found it. It just needs . . .' She stopped and smiled, 'Well, let's just say it's a surprise and will be ready for you tomorrow.'

'Thank you,' said Anneli. 'Thank you very much indeed.'

And, feeling shy, she turned and fled.

★ ★ ★

Anne Fine

The next morning, Anneli left early for school. Something was bothering her, something about the boring old painting above the fireplace. There was something *wrong* about it, Anneli was sure. What it was, she had no idea; but it was bothering her terribly.

Usually, she was so late she had to dash straight past the gates to Carrington Lodge without time for so much as a glance between the iron bars. Today, she stopped and peered through, taking her time, wondering. The garden looked more vivid somehow, in the sharp morning light. The lawns gleamed with freshness. The row of holly trees stood tall, like sentries guarding the wall behind from attack. It was the same as ever, but something was wrong.

Whatever it was, it haunted Anneli all day. Henry became bored with her constant fretting, and irritated with having to nudge her to finish her work so that he could turn over the pages of the book they were sharing. All day, the sheets of paper Anneli was writing on kept blurring, and suddenly she'd see, as clearly as if it were there in front of her, Tom's last real painting. The page of her own writing would sharpen again, blotting it out, then, almost at once, blur into what she'd seen as she peered between the bars that morning.

What was wrong? What was wrong? The holly trees were taller, of course. But that's to be expected. Trees grow.

Trees grow, to be sure. But only in height. Not in number!

Six hollies. Seven. Which? Oh, *which*?

Six holly trees in the garden. And seven in the painting. *Surely* the painting hanging over the fireplace had seven. *Surely* only six grew in the garden. No painter worth his salt made that sort of mistake. Certainly not Tom, with his eye for detail and his great skill at copying things accurately. Either Anneli herself must have made a mistake in the counting, or there was a mystery here to be solved. And Anneli didn't believe that she was mistaken. After all, hadn't Mrs Pears herself said to Anneli only the day before: 'You're sharp enough to be an

Anne Fine

art historian!'

Anneli could scarcely contain herself until the bell rang. At three-fifteen precisely, she grabbed Henry's arm and dragged him along with her, under the shadow of the walls of Carrington Lodge. They reached the gates and stood side by side, staring inside.

'So?' Henry demanded. 'So?'

'Don't you *see*?' Anneli cried. 'Only six holly trees!'

'So?'

'So Tom put *seven* in his painting.'

'So?'

'So!'

'Maybe he had forgotten how many there were.'

Anneli's lip curled scornfully.

'Don't be so silly. He grew up here.'

Henry's brow puckered. Anneli was right. No one could grow up in a garden and not know its trees. He scuffed his shoes against the kerb, and sighed.

'Have to get in and look, then. But only

after you've climbed back through that roof tunnel and counted the hollies on that painting again. I'm not going to get caught trespassing for nothing. I'll meet you back here in an hour.'

Anneli nodded. She wasn't keen, but she knew it made sense.

Henry took off down his own street.

'You mind you count them properly, Anneli Kuukka,' he called back over his shoulder. 'Use your fingers.'

And Anneli was so grateful that he'd as good as promised to go trespassing with her, she didn't even run after and thump him.

They met an hour later. When Anneli arrived, Henry was already waiting, squatting on the kerb-side. Anneli walked up and stood in front of him. 'I crawled back through the roof tunnel as quietly as I could. Mrs Pears wasn't anywhere to be seen and so I got a good long look at the painting. And there are seven holly trees.' She lifted her fingers, one by one. 'One, two, three, four, five, six, *seven*.'

Henry sighed heavily, and rose to his feet.

'A promise is a promise,' he admitted. 'But you go first.'

The gates proved easy to climb. Wrought iron has advantages. It was one curly foothold after another, all the way up and all the way down on the other side.

'We could walk up the drive and say we're collecting for a new Art Room,' Anneli suggested.

'You must be *joking*,' Henry said, and dragged her with him into the shadow of the shrubbery. They picked their way through the dense undergrowth. Wet leaves slapped Anneli's ankles, and prickly bushes scraped at the elbows she lifted to protect herself. But gradually the thick green gloom became more and more flecked with silver, and then wide shafts of sunlight were spilling between the last lilacs, and they had reached the edge of the old cobbled stable yard.

Here they stopped and considered.

Anneli the Art Hater

'Well,' Henry said. 'What do you think? You're the expert.'

'Expert?'

'At getting inside the mind of the villain,' Henry explained. 'Like in Sherlock Holmes. You being, like Tom, an accomplished forger.'

Anneli ignored the insult. She stood and stared at the line of holly trees, thinking in silence.

It was an art historian's job to work things out from little clues. What possible reason could Tom have had for painting in an extra tree? Was he trying to hide something? What? He sent a message with the painting. *For Clarrie. All I own. Best Love. Tom.* What could be clearer than that? It *must* be his sovereigns. But all there was in front of her was solid wall and great tall holly trees.

Wait a minute! This painting was over fifty years old. How much did hollies grow each year? And which tree was the extra one? And who says walls are always solid?

Suddenly Anneli stepped forward into the sunlight. Henry reached out to pull her back to the shadows and safety, but she shook him off. She was filled with excitement. Making a huge effort of concentration, she called Tom's painting to mind. It formed obediently and immediately inside her head.

'There!' she said, pointing. 'We should be looking at that part of the wall there. That's where he painted in the extra tree.'

Henry stepped forward.

'All right, then. Let's look.'

He led the way across to the stables, and pushed open the upper half of the door. In the dim light the two of them could see the old horse stalls overflowing with clutter: broken old wheelchairs, half a bicycle, rusty bedsprings and an ancient washing machine, a wheelbarrow, boxes and flower-pots and – right at the very end – a long wooden ladder.

Together, and keeping their voices as low as it is possible whilst squabbling, Anneli and Henry dragged the heavy ladder out into the stable yard. They laid it on the cobbles to rest for a moment. Then, taking up each end again, they carried it towards the wall.

'Mind!' Henry grumbled. 'Stop shoving. Hollies are *prickly*!'

'Mind *yourself*!' Anneli snapped. She was getting quite tense. Several windows overlooked the stable yard. It was quite possible that someone was watching.

Henry laid his end of the ladder down on the cobbles. Anneli raised hers. Henry came over to add his strength to hers. Together they heaved the ladder up against the wall.

'Further along,' Anneli told him. 'It should be further along, between these two trees.'

Henry scraped the ladder along the wall.

'There!' Anneli cried. 'Stop there *exactly*.'

Henry laid his foot on the first rung of the ladder.

'No you don't,' Anneli told him. 'This is *my* something precious.'

She gasped, and rushed up the ladder before he could begin to argue.

The holly trees on either side had grown so high and spread so wide that she was climbing

up into a mass of leaves. It was dark. The fiendish prickles dug through her clothing and caught her hair. She spread her fingers out to feel the wall, and was reminded suddenly of when she first spread her fingers in just the same way to feel the little wooden door in the wall that led to Mrs Pears and all of this.

The stone wall was rough and chilled, and slightly slimy.

'Anything?' called Henry.

'Not yet,' she shouted down. How tall had Tom painted the tree? That was a clue. A little bit taller, she was sure. She'd have to go higher.

'I'm going up.'

'I'm holding on.'

Anneli went higher. She reached up as far as she could. The fingers of one hand suddenly slid over a little ledge.

'I'm going one rung higher.'

'Anything?'

Anneli's whole hand disappeared.

'It's a hole. There's a hole in the wall. A square hole.'

Anne Fine

'How big?'

Anneli felt its contours.

'About the same size as – as – a bread bin.'

It was the only thing that size that came to mind.

'It's probably a dove hole. Watch out. There might be pigeons inside.'

'There's no pigeons inside,' said Anneli. 'It's all blocked up. No, it isn't. It isn't blocked up at all. It's filled up. There's something in it. And it's a *box*.'

Her heart turned over from excitement. She pulled. The little box slid easily towards her, stirring a dank smell of leaf-mould. She tugged it closer. Then, feeling her way back on to the lower rung where she felt safer, she drew the box out of the hole in the wall where it had rested undisturbed and waited safely for so many years, and hugged it to her chest.

'I'm coming down now.'

She backed down through the mass of prickly leaves, clutching the box tightly, until she reached the ground. Henry was jumping from one foot to another. He reached out and took the box from her, and turned it round so that the clasp was facing Anneli.

The clasp was stiff, and a little tricky. It took Anneli a moment or two to lift it. Henry stood by in silence. Then Anneli slowly raised the grimy lid. Inside there lay a thick purple velvet cloth, hiding whatever was beneath. Anneli reached in and began to unfold it.

'Josh would love that,' Henry observed. 'He needs a new cloth. That one he's got is practically *threadbare*.'

'She'll give it to him,' Anneli said. 'I'm sure she will.'

The purple cloth lay folded back, revealing a pool of old sovereigns, inches deep. Anneli dipped her finger in and stirred. The coins shifted out of their long sleep uneasily, clinking with resentment.

Anneli picked one out, and bit it, hard.

'He was a forger,' she explained. 'Just our luck if he was a counterfeiter, too.'

'Solid?'

Anne Fine

'Quite solid.'

'Unlike the wall.' Henry looked up into the leafy mass of holly, a little puzzled. 'It must have taken years and years for these trees to grow wide and high enough to hide that hole in the wall. I can't understand why no one worked it out before. His sister had more clues than you, and it was her garden.'

'She wasn't thinking,' Anneli said. 'She was – bereft.'

They looked at one another over the box without speaking. Then Anneli gently closed the lid.

'It's not ours,' she reminded Henry.

'Pity,' said Henry. 'You deserve it. You were the one to notice the puzzle in the painting, and you were the one to solve it. I've never known you take such an interest in art, Anneli Kuukka. In fact, I've always thought of you as an art hater.'

'I am an art hater,' said Anneli. 'I'm just more choosy than I used to be about the bits of art I hate.'

CHAPTER NINE

Anneli carried the Running-Away Box up the garden path to Mrs Pears' front door. Balancing it in the crook of one arm, she rang the bell. Mrs Pears seemed to take an age to answer; and by the time she did, Anneli's plans to tell the news gently had dissolved entirely in her excitement.

'See!' she said, laying the box down on the hall table. 'See what I found! Surprise, surprise!'

Mrs Pears gasped, and Anneli knew from the look on her face that even after so many years she'd recognised the little rosewood box at once.

Surprise indeed! Mrs Pears ran her fingertips over the tarnished silver shield with T. W. H. C-S. engraved upon it. A small tear glistened at the corner of her eye. Even before she lifted the lid, she was crying gently.

Anneli leaned over and tipped the sovereigns out on to the table.

'See?' she said. 'Hidden at the bottom. A
letter from Tom. To you.'

It was faded and stained. But written quite
clearly on the front in that old-fashioned curly
handwriting was: *For Clarrie*.

'He certainly cared about you,' said Anneli.
'I'm not sure that either Henry or Josh would
ever bother to write a letter to me. But then

again, I wouldn't sit still for them in a prickly dress to be painted, like you did.'

She slipped away upstairs, before the tears could fall faster, to fetch down Tom's last proper painting. She wanted to explain to Mrs Pears just how she had first noticed that there was a mystery, and how she had later worked out the puzzle. She pushed open the door to the room full of paintings. Though it was filled with evening light, from the moment she stepped in she had the sense that she was being watched and, nervously, she left the door open.

Anneli looked round at all the paintings. Horses still cantered down leafy lanes. Water droplets still spun in sunlight over waterfalls. Ladies still strolled arm in arm between roses. Anneli gave herself a sensible shake. No one was here. No one was watching.

Carrying the little wooden desk chair over to the fireplace, she climbed up to reach Tom's last painting and lift it down. Gently she lowered it to the floor, and then jumped from the chair. Again the sense of being watched swept over her and, quickly, she spun around.

There, still leaning against the legs of the desk on the other side of the room, was the painting of Clarrie sitting on the garden bench in the white dress, clutching the rabbit. Anneli stared. It was so strange to think that Clarrie and Mrs Pears were one and the same.

The pale, grave, little face stared back.

Anneli suddenly said aloud:

'That's how he saw you, isn't it? And that's how he must have remembered you later, when he was scared and miles from home.'

She came a little closer. It was a fine painting. Every pearl button on the frilly dress was gleaming. Clarrie's hair glinted in the sunlight. The rabbit's fur shone.

'If I had any money,' Anneli told Clarrie, 'and if you were not too precious to be sold, I'd buy you for myself since I'm not really much of an art hater any longer.'

She picked up Tom's last painting and turned to leave. Just as she did so, Mrs Pears appeared in the open doorway. All signs of tears had disappeared. Her old face was glowing. Smiling, she stepped in and swung the door back on its hinges behind her. And there, suspended from a clothes hanger and hanging in dreamy white billows and flounces and gathers and ruffles, was Clarrie's best dress, the dress in the painting, the dress from that summer long, long ago.

'I wanted you to have it,' said Mrs Pears. 'I know it's prickly round the neck and you won't ever want to wear it. But still I wanted you to have it.'

Anneli reached out and took a pleat of the material between her fingers.

'It's beautiful,' she said. 'Quite beautiful. It's something precious.'

And she did wear it. She wore it all one sunny summer afternoon, sitting on the bench in the garden of Carrington Lodge. The dress was hot and heavy to wear, and prickly round the neck, but Anneli sat upright and still, running

her fingers down the fur of Henry's black and white rabbit, keeping him happy in her lap. Around her, behind two wide semi-circles of easels, children were busy painting. Some stood, some sat on chairs, some were strapped into wheelchairs; but all were working hard, frowning with concentration, sucking the ends of their brushes as they thought, or squinting around the edges of their easels.

It had, of course, been Henry's idea: a painting competition at Carrington Lodge's Summer Fair. Tom's painting would be propped up beside the bench to encourage everyone who entered. Mrs Pears would judge the winner. And at the end of the afternoon there would be a Grand Auction of all the paintings in aid of the new school art room.

'Who'd buy them?' Anneli asked sceptically.

'Mothers,' said Henry. 'Mothers and fathers and grannies. You wait and see.'

As usual, Henry was right. Straight after the judging, Jodie climbed on the wooden ramp that came with the brand new minibus

Anne Fine

Mrs Pears bought with money from Tom's sovereigns. She held up the first of the paintings – the one done by Josh. Anneli stared. She looked, she thought, like a dirty white maggot with stick legs. The grass was grey and covered with thumbprints. The rabbit was a large splodge in the sky.

'What am I offered,' Jodie asked the crowd, 'for this very fine painting?'

Henry opened the bidding by offering ten pence. Helen bid thirty. Henry and Helen bid against one another till Henry dropped out at two pounds fifty after catching a rather stern look from Miss Pears. Helen bid ten pence more, and just as she began to smile triumphantly, Jodie broke the only rule of auctioneering that Anneli knew by bidding ten pence more than that and promptly bringing down the hammer.

'Two pounds seventy for that,' said a very complacent Henry. 'Not bad.'

Josh stood by shyly and proudly, pressing his new velvet cloth to his cheek.

Anneli the Art Hater

Anneli said suspiciously to Henry:

'I never knew you still had two pounds fifty.'

'I don't,' said Henry. 'I am penniless.'

'But you just bid that much for Josh's painting. It might have been knocked down to you.'

Henry stared.

'Knocked down to me? What? With his mother standing there?' He snorted loudly. 'I was just doing my bit to raise the proceeds a little.'

'What a great fizzing *cheat*!'

Henry regarded Anneli with lofty disdain.

'There's a lot more to art than you think, Anneli Kuukka.'

And he lifted his hand to enter the bidding for the next painting.

Anneli looked at it. It was even worse than Josh's. Her eyes looked like giant nostrils. The dress was one large shapeless blob. The rabbit was falling off the edge of the paper.

Mrs Pears came up, resting on Miss Pears' arm.

'That's truly awful,' she remarked to her daughter. 'A pity your grandfather isn't still living. He would have bid a lot for that painting.'

But even as it was, with a bit of help from Henry surreptitiously bidding behind their backs, the painting went for over three pounds.

Anneli was still standing scandalised when the photographer from the local newspaper came over to take her picture. Obediently she seated herself once again on the bench, the rabbit in her lap, Tom's painting propped beside her.

Henry ran forward to shake out the frills in her dress. A smile crossed Mrs Pears' face, as though she were remembering something private and pleasant, and long ago.

The photographer focused her lens. Here was a lovely photograph, she thought, but for the little girl looking so fierce.

In order to distract her, she said:

'Anneli, you must be quite a little art lover – '

She was astonished when they all burst out laughing.